This book belongs to:

Amanda Anderson___

Victoria Plum

Victoria Gives
a
Flying Lesson

Angela Rippon

PURNELL

SBN 361 05060 7
Text copyright © 1981 Daredevils Limited
Illustrations copyright © 1981 Purnell and Sons Limited
'Victoria Plum' copyright © 1981 W.N. Sharpe Limited
Published 1981 by Purnell Books, Berkshire House, Queen Street, Maidenhead, Berkshire
Made and printed in Great Britain by Purnell and Sons Limited, Paulton (Bristol) and London

"Atishoo," sneezed poor Victoria Plum, "atishoo, atishoo!" She sat down on a stool for a moment. "Oh dear," she said to herself, "all the dust and cobwebs are tickling my nose and I can't stop sneezing." Then, as if to prove the point, she burst into another loud "atishoo" which echoed round and round her snug little sitting room. Victoria was the youngest of the woodland fairies. She was a tidy fairy, and always kept her tree house as bright as a new pin. Each spring, however, when the sunshine filtered into her home after the long, dark winter days, Victoria felt that everything needed an extra bit of polish and sparkle to start the new year with a fresh face.

That morning, Victoria covered her long, dark curls in a huge cap, wrapped her best apron around her dress, and busied herself with broom and duster in every corner. "Now that spring has come at last," she said to herself, "I really must get on with all my spring cleaning." Right in the middle of the morning, when she had barely cleaned half the house, Benjamin knocked on the door and strolled in. Benjamin, or Ben as his friends called him, was an elf who lived a few trees away. Victoria was always pleased to see him, but today she was much too busy to gossip. "Do stay and make yourself at home, Ben," she said without stopping her work, "but I am afraid I can't stop. I really must finish my spring cleaning."

Ben could not believe his ears. "Why do you bother?" he asked. "It's such a waste of effort. After all you are a fairy, so why don't you magic everything clean? I know I would."

Victoria knew very well what Ben would do if his house needed spring cleaning. He was one of Victoria's closest friends, but he was an elf and, as everyone knows, elves do not like work. Ben spent his time visiting friends, playing his flute, and enjoying himself. Whenever anything cropped up that he did not like he simply used his magic to make it disappear. Ben just could not understand why Victoria insisted on doing everything the hard way, and he could not bear to watch his friend hard at work when all he wanted to do was chat! "If you won't use your magic," he said, "let me use mine."

"Oh, no," said Victoria. "That would be cheating. Besides, I like spring cleaning," and with that she disappeared in a cloud of dust and burst into yet another fit of sneezing.

"You are impossible," said Ben grumpily, "but I am not going to give up. If you won't let me magic away the housework, at least let me cure your sneezing."

"Certainly not," replied Victoria. "We both know what happened the last time you tried that spell." Ben remembered the fun he had had trying to cure Mole of his sneezing, and he laughed till the tears ran down his cheeks. Although she thought she should not, Victoria could not help laughing too.

Mole was friendly with everyone in the Great Wood. He was always burrowing about, in a hurry to be somewhere else. However busy he was, he would stop to say a cheery hello whenever he met a friend. Unfortunately his friends did not see him very often because Mole liked nothing better than to burrow his way under the soft earth, making long, winding tunnels that criss-crossed all over the floor of the Great Wood.

Underground Mole was happy. He knew every inch of his dark, private world, and his sensitive nose would twitch with pleasure at the smell of the damp earth. "Ah," Mole would say, "home." Above ground, it was a different story. Mole's black button eyes were little use in daylight. He was so shortsighted that his friends had to shout, "Hello, Mole" whenever they saw him so that he would not bump into them. That was not the worst problem, however. Mole's delicate nose could not stand the fresh air. It made him sneeze. He did not sneeze once, or twice, or even three times, but over and over again. It was especially bad in the summer. The tiny grains of pollen that floated on the breeze from flower to flower tickled his nose and made him sneeze fit to burst.

"Hay fever," Mole would say cheerfully, but the worse it became, the more determined his woodland friends were to cure him.

"We'll ask the fairies to help," they decided, and went in search of Victoria.

Unfortunately for Mole,
Victoria was out that day, so
Mole's friends asked Ben to help. Now
Ben had just been given a new flute, and
was not paying attention while he cast his
spell. When he had finished, Mole had stopped
sneezing, but he had started hiccuping instead.
Poor Mole. Ben's spell made everything worse. At
least when he had a fit of sneezing he could escape by
going underground, but the hiccups followed him
everywhere. In fact they were even worse underground.
They came with such force that he kept bumping his head
on the roof and rolling down the long tunnels. This gave
Mole such a headache that for the first time in his life he
looked miserable. Eventually the blue tit said, "The only
person who can help is Victoria," and he went to find her.
Victoria found the strongest spell she could in her magic
books. Then she crossed her fingers for luck. She
concentrated hard, sprinkled fairy dust over Mole's
twitchy nose, and whispered the secret fairy words.
Everyone waited, hardly daring to breathe, then,
"Hiccup. Hicc-shoo. Atishoo! How marvellous," cried
Mole, "I can – atishoo – sneeze again," and with a
scattering of earth and a burst of "atishoos" he
disappeared happily underground. Victoria
had intended to cure Mole's hay fever and
hiccups, but she was a novice fairy, so
her spells did not always turn out
right. But Mole was happy,
so that was enough.

As Ben was the cause of Mole's problems, Victoria did not want him to put a spell on her! Ben was bored watching Victoria work while he did nothing, so he took out his flute. "There is something I can do for you," he said. "I'll play my flute and then you'll have music while you work." When Ben began to play, the air was filled with a strange, squeaky noise as the notes tumbled from the flute without melody or tune. Ben thought it was the coolest, sweetest music he had ever played. Victoria thought it was awful. She would not dream of hurting his feelings by asking him to stop playing, so she allowed herself a tiny piece of magic. In her imagination she turned the squawky noise into beautiful music and she smiled. Ben was delighted that he had pleased his friend at last, and he played with extra enthusiasm. That made the noise even worse, but inside her head Victoria could hear only the prettiest of tunes, and she finished her work in no time.

When the last book was dusted and the broom returned to its cupboard, Victoria took off her apron and cap and folded them away. Then she realised that her hard work had made her very hungry.

"What I would like now is a refreshing cup of blackberry juice and a nice bowl of rose hip salad," she said. "Would you like to stay to tea, Ben?" Ben knew what a marvellous cook Victoria was, and he was at the tea table before Victoria could even blink.

The table was a large round log. Victoria had found it after some men had come to cut down a dead tree. The top was perfectly smooth and had a beautiful pattern of circles which grew smaller towards the centre. One of the older fairies explained that each circle marked a year in the life of the tree. There were nearly a hundred rings, and Victoria loved the pattern they made. Ben liked the log table because it was big, and a big table always holds more food than a small one! While she prepared the tea, Victoria was thinking how lovely her home looked, and how lucky she was to live in the rambling old house nestling under the roots of the huge beech tree on the edge of the Great Wood. The walls of her house were covered with the delicate patterns of soft green moss, and each room had a high curved ceiling made by the tree's roots as they arched their way down into the earth. Victoria's sitting room and kitchen were at the front where the sun sprinkled its warmth and light through the ferns which grew outside. Her bedroom overlooked a garden of wild flowers, while the cool corridors that ran deep into the heart of the tree made perfect store rooms. Here Victoria kept her food, and her most precious possessions: her favourite hats, her best winter coat, the silvery-white tablecloth the caterpillars had woven for her birthday and, most important of all, her fairy books and potions.

The tree grew out of an old stone wall. There were so many nooks and crannies in the wall that it made a perfect home for all sorts of woodland creatures. Doormice lived there, frogs and toads, spiders and snails, rabbits and lizards. These, and many others, had homes tucked away in the crevices between the stones. It was like living in a block of flats, and Victoria loved it. With so many friends close by she could never be lonely as there was always someone dropping in to say hello.

Suddenly, Victoria's daydream was interrupted. The blue tit burst into the room and tumbled in a heap on the floor. His feathers were ruffled and he was quite out of breath. He was so excited that his message came jumbling out in a breathless muddle and the only words Victoria could understand were "cat" and "Baby Robin". Eventually she calmed him down enough to understand the reason for his panic. One of the baby robins had fallen out of its nest, and the cat who lived in the big house was lying flat in the long grass waiting to grab the little bird.

"And it's only a matter of seconds before he pounces!" said the blue tit dramatically. Victoria knew exactly where the robins had built their nest in a thick hedge near the bottom of the garden. Without wasting another moment she flew off through the trees as fast as her tiny wings would carry her, leaving Ben with his mouth full of hazelnut cake.

As she flew towards the hedge, Victoria could see the parent birds diving on the cat and twittering at her to leave their baby alone. Then she spotted the cat crouching low in the grass, tail flicking, whiskers twitching. She could not see the little baby robin anywhere. "Oh, don't say I've come too late," she whispered. Then she saw the tiny bird. His baby feathers of speckled brown had made him almost invisible against the earth. Victoria heaved a sigh of relief and settled on a primrose a little way away. She whispered to him to stay quite still while she tried to work out what to do. It was no use trying to frighten the cat away. The robins had already tried that without success. "I know," she thought, "I'll drop a sleeping potion in her eyes and make her fall asleep just long enough . . . Oh, you silly, empty-headed fairy," she said out loud, as she remembered that all her potions were back at home and in her hurry to get to the nest she had left everything behind. "It would take too long to go back," she muttered. "I must do something now." Suddenly Victoria had a marvellous idea. "Oh yes," she cried, with relief. "He's bound to help." Just as she was about to fly off, Ben turned up. He was never one to hurry, and he had stayed to finish his hazelnut cake at Victoria's house. "Stay with the baby robin," she called to him, "to give him courage, and while I'm away do something to distract the cat."

"Like what?" said Ben.

"I don't know," called Victoria. "You're the one who always has bright ideas for playing practical jokes. You think of something." Before Ben could take another breath, Victoria had flown off through the flowers.

"Don't be too long," he shouted after her. "I don't like the cat much either." Ben looked at the cat and he shuddered. Then he thought of all the new tricks he could try out and he smiled. He would not be unkind, but he would make sure the cat was so busy trying to get rid of him that she would not think about the baby robin.

Ben landed lightly on the cat's head, then started running up and down her back, swinging round her tail and playing leap frog over her ears. The poor cat did not know what was happening. She rolled on her back and lashed out with her paws to try to get rid of Ben, but the elf just buzzed round her head like a noisy fly. He bounced across her nose using her whiskers as a springboard. He made faces at her until she went cross-eyed, and he tickled her tummy until she was helpless with laughter. Ben could not remember when he had had so much fun, but however hard he worked, the cat stayed just close enough to pounce on the robin. After ten minutes of jumping and tickling Ben was worn out. He ducked inside a daffodil to rest. "I don't know where you've gone, Victoria," he puffed, "but if you don't come back soon I shall run out of ideas!"

Victoria had flown in search of Mr P., the kind, old gardener at the big house. He fed all the birds and knew where they hid their nests. When he found the robins' nest, the very first nest that spring, he took a special interest and kept the cat away. After searching everywhere, Victoria finally spotted his bright red hat bobbing above the fence of the vegetable patch. She fluttered over the fence and landed on Mr P.'s hat.

"I wonder how my robins are today," she whispered in his ear. It was the gentlest of fairy whispers to make Mr P. believe he had thought the words himself, but he took no notice and went on planting lettuces. "I wonder how my robins are today," whispered Victoria again, but still Mr P. went on planting. "Oh, do listen," urged Victoria, almost in despair. This time the gardener sat back and said, "I haven't seen my robins today. I wonder how they are." "At last," sighed Victoria, flying after Mr P. who was already striding down the garden. Before he had even reached the hedge he saw the cat rolling on the grass. He could not see Ben, of course, because elves and fairies are almost always invisible to humans, but his sharp eyes saw the robins and their baby, and he guessed what was happening.

"Oh, no you don't, my beauty," he said, scooping the cat into his arms. "I'll put you out of harm's way," and to the relief of everyone, he carried the cat away.

As soon as Mr P. had
gone they began coaxing the
robin to fly back to the safety of the
nest, but he was so scared that he could not
move a muscle. Neither Victoria nor Ben had
the sort of powerful magic that can make birds
fly, and no matter how hard they tried they could
not make the baby bird move. At last Victoria said,
"There is only one thing to do, Ben. You and I will
have to carry him back." Ben gasped and was about to
object, but Victoria looked determined so he said nothing.
They stood on either side of the bird, linked their arms
underneath his body, and gently lifted him off the ground.
"If you ask me," panted Ben as they struggled upwards,
"little birds eat too much. He's heavy." Victoria could not
answer. The robin was very heavy and she needed all her
breath to carry him. Her tiny wings worked harder than
they had ever done before. Every moment the bird felt
heavier, and poor Victoria thought her arms would break.
"We'll never do it. I can't keep this up," she puffed.
"Nor me," gulped Ben, and he gave the robin a prod
in the ribs. "Silly bird. You should be able to fly on
your own without all this fuss." The little robin
did not like being prodded, so he flapped his
wings a little to make himself comfortable.
"Go on," encouraged Victoria. "Flap a bit
more and you will fly." The robin
flapped his fat little wings harder,
and with a jerk and a flutter
he flew into the nest.

Ben and Victoria both tumbled in an exhausted heap. While they caught their breath, the robins fussed over their naughty baby. "We don't know how to thank you," they said. "What can we do to repay your kindness?" Ben was an elf who never missed an opportunity. "Well, there is something I would like," he said. "As you know I play the flute rather well, but I've always admired your beautiful singing. Would you teach me some of your songs so that I can play them on my flute?" Mr Robin was delighted to be paid such a generous compliment. It was true, he did have a beautiful voice, and in the summer he filled the woods with his lovely songs. "I'd be happy to teach you," he said. "Come again in June when the youngsters have left home, and I'll have plenty of time to sing for you." Ben was thrilled. He said goodbye to his friends, then promptly fell fast asleep on the branch! "There must be a way of saying a special thank you to you, Victoria," said the robins, but Victoria did not want any reward. She had been happy to help and that was enough, but she was too tired to argue. Without another word, the robins tucked their heads under their wings and plucked the softest, whitest down feathers Victoria had ever seen. "Why they are perfect," she cried. "Thank you. They are just what I need to make a warm collar for my best winter coat. What a lovely end to a tiring day."